My Two Feet

My Two Feet

story by Alice Schertle
pictures by Meredith Dunham

Lothrop,
Lee & Shepard
Books
New York

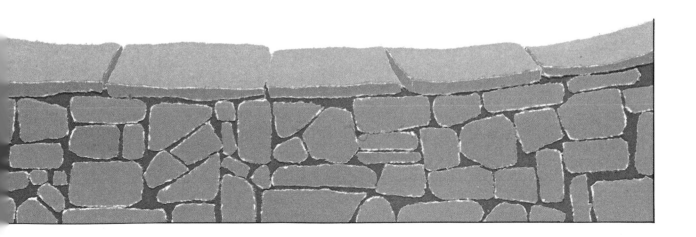

Also by Alice Schertle and Meredith Dunham
In My Treehouse

Library of Congress Cataloging in Publication Data
Schertle, Alice.
   My two feet.
   Summary: A young girl describes the adventures she has with her
two feet, shod and unshod, year round.
   1. Children's stories, American.   [1. Foot—Fiction]
I. Dunham, Meredith, ill.   II. Title.
PZ7.S3442My   1985   [E]   84-12192
ISBN 0-688-02676-1   ISBN 0-688-02677-X (lib. bdg.)

To my mother and father—A.S.

For my mother—M.D.

My two feet like to walk in special places, like on stepping-stones, on top of a wall, in a pile of leaves, and in all the squares on the sidewalk, but not the cracks.

When there's music on the radio, my two
feet want to dance. I dance around and
around and around. I get so dizzy I fall down
on the floor. Then the whole room seems to
go around and around and around.

My two feet love summertime. That's when
I don't wear shoes at all. On my two bare feet
I can run like the wind. I can jump a mile.
And I can climb like a monkey. I hold on with
my fingers, and with my toes, too.

Sometimes in summer the cement is too hot to stand on, except in the shade. One day my mom said it was so hot you could fry an egg on the sidewalk. I know that doesn't work, because I tried it. The egg didn't cook at all, but my cat liked it anyway.

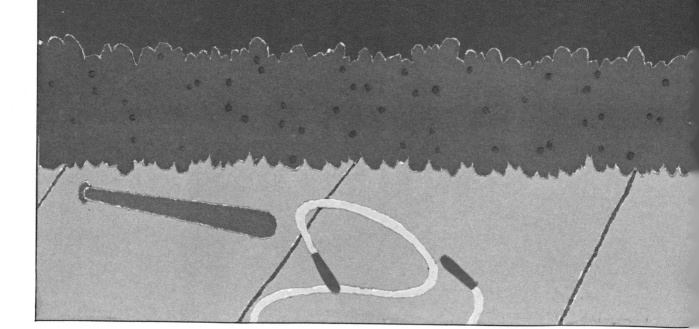

My cat walks very softly, because she's always barefoot. When I'm barefoot, I can walk softly, too. Even my cat doesn't hear me.

Sometimes going barefoot can be dangerous, like the time I stepped on a bee. My dad took the stinger out with tweezers. He told me bees die when they sting somebody. I felt sorry for my bee, even though my foot hurt.

Last summer I
stepped on a piece of
glass. The doctor sewed
my foot with four
stitches. I had to wear a
big bandage and walk
with a cane my brother
made out of a mop. This
summer I'm going to
watch out for glass.
And bees.

LEMONADE
15¢

When I go barefoot, my two feet get so dirty I have to stay off the new carpet in the living room. If I have to put on shoes to go somewhere, my mom makes me wash my feet. I tell her no one can see inside my shoes. She says <u>she</u> would know my feet are dirty, and that's enough.

The beach is the best place to be barefoot. When I walk at the beach, my two feet sink deep in the sand. I make a long line of footprints, right down to the water. There are lots of seagulls making seagull prints, too.

I stand where the waves can come up to my ankles. When the water swishes back out it tickles my feet and washes away everybody's tracks. Then I make some more footprints, and so do the seagulls.

When summer is over and it starts to get cold, I have to wear shoes every day. In the morning it takes longer to get dressed, because when I look for my shoes, one of them is always missing. Sometimes I find it under the bed or in the bathroom. When I sneak up on my cat with shoes on my feet, she hears me each time. And everybody is always saying, "Your shoelace is untied."

Shoes are a lot of trouble.

When I put on my old shoes, they always feel too tight. My toes touch the end. So my mom has to take me to the store to buy new ones. We walk to the bus stop and I say, "These old shoes are taking their last walk."

My mom says, "I hope they make it."

The shoe lady measures my feet. I show her which shoes I want to try on. My mom says, "Be sure they're big enough. This one grows like a weed."

When I try on my shoes, the shoe lady tells me to wiggle my toes. My mom asks if my toes feel the end. I walk over to the mirror to see how I look in my new shoes.

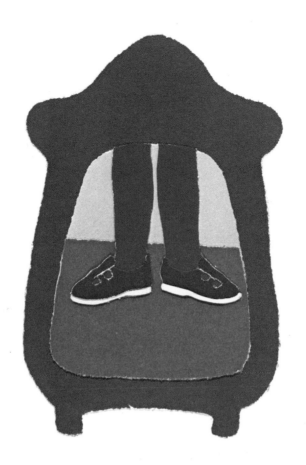

I carry my old, tired shoes home in a box. My two feet feel funny inside my new ones. All the way home I keep looking down, and I'm careful not to scuff the toes.

If you have to wear shoes, new shoes are nice.

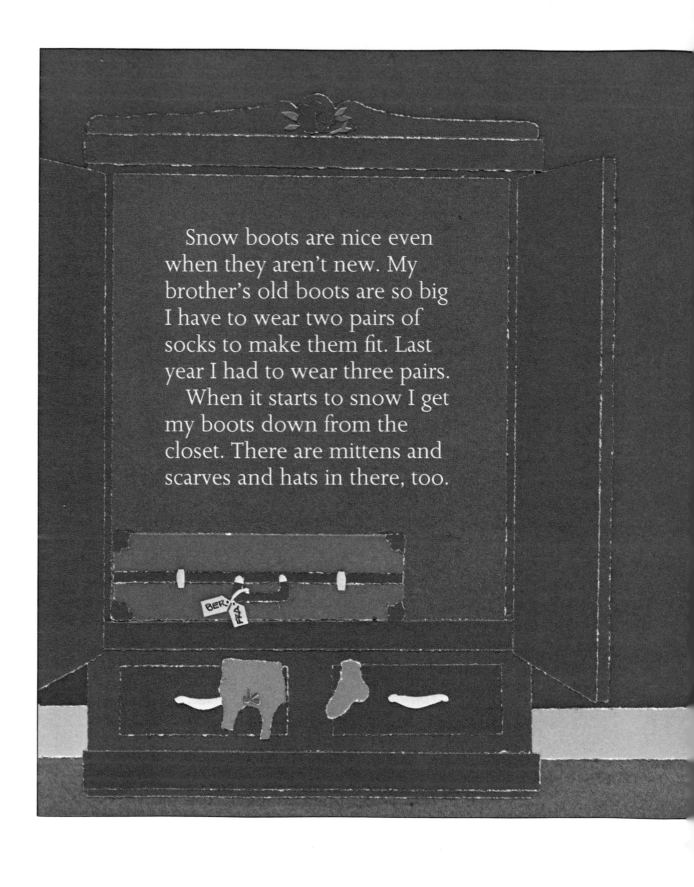

Snow boots are nice even
when they aren't new. My
brother's old boots are so big
I have to wear two pairs of
socks to make them fit. Last
year I had to wear three pairs.

When it starts to snow I get
my boots down from the
closet. There are mittens and
scarves and hats in there, too.

Then, all bundled up, I go outside. If the
snow is just right, my boots make a crunchy
noise wherever I walk.

My cat doesn't like snow. She picks up her
paws, shakes them, and runs back in the house.

I stay out and play. New snow is so soft I can
sink in it up to my knees. But if snow gets in over
the tops of my boots, pretty soon my two feet are
freezing. Then I run back in the house, too.

I pull off my boots and sit by the fire until my feet are toasty warm. My mom makes hot chocolate to toast my insides.

In snowy winter and sunny summer, my two feet take me wherever I want to go. In new shoes and old boots, and on my two bare feet, I dance and hop and jump and kick, I climb and slide and walk and run, until my two feet need a rest.

And so do I.